My First Pocket Guide

Wisconsin

By Carole Marsh

Correlates with Wisconsin's MODEL Academic Standards for Social Studies

The Wisconsin Experience

The GALLOPADE GANG

Carole Marsh
Bob Longmeyer
Chad Beard
Cecil Anderson
Steven Saint-Laurent
Karin Petersen
Billie Walburn
Doug Boston
Jill Sanders
William Nesbitt, Jr.
Kathy Zimmer
Wanda Coats
Terry Briggs
Jackie Clayton
Pam Dufresne
Cranston Davenport
Lisa Stanley
Antoinette Miller
Victoria DeJoy
Tena Simpson

Published by GALLOPADE INTERNATIONAL

www.thewisconsinexperience.com
800-536-2GET • www.gallopade.com

Gallopade is proud to be a member of these educational organizations and associations:

NSSEA

ASCD

SHOPA MEMBER
School, Home, & Office Products Association

Other Wisconsin Experience Products

- The Wisconsin Experience!
- The BIG Wisconsin Reproducible Activity Book
- The Wisconsin Coloring Book
- My First Book About Wisconsin!
- Wisconsin "Jography": A Fun Run Through Our State
- Wisconsin Jeopardy!: Answers and Questions About Our State
- The Wisconsin Experience! Sticker Pack
- The Wisconsin Experience! Poster/Map
- Discover Wisconsin CD-ROM
- Wisconsin "Geo" Bingo Game
- Wisconsin "Histo" Bingo Game

A Word From the Author... (okay, a few words)...

Hi!

Here's your own handy pocket guide about the great state of Wisconsin! It really will fit in a pocket–I tested it. And it really will be useful when you want to know a fact you forgot, to bone up for a test, or when your teacher says, "I wonder . . ." and you have the answer–instantly! Wow, I'm impressed!

Get smart, have fun!

Carole Marsh

Wisconsin Basics explores your state's symbols and their special meanings!

Wisconsin Geography digs up the what's where in your state!

Wisconsin History is like traveling through time to some of your state's great moments!

Wisconsin People introduces you to famous personalities and your next-door neighbors!

Wisconsin Places shows you where you might enjoy your next family vacation!

Wisconsin Nature - no preservatives here, just what Mother Nature gave to Wisconsin!

All the real fun stuff that we just HAD to save for its own section!

Who Named You?

Wisconsin's official state name is...

Wisconsin

Word Definition

OFFICIAL: appointed, authorized, or approved by a government or organization

Wisconsin will be on one of the commemorative state quarters issued in 2004. Look for it in cash registers everywhere!

Statehood: May 29, 1848

Wisconsin was the 30th state to join the Union.

Wisconsin's Native Name!

Wisconsin is named for the Wisconsin River, which was named by the Native Americans. Their word was *weeskonsan*, which means "the gathering of waters."

Other place names taken from Native American words include Wausaukee, Menasha, Menomonie, and Manitowish.

What's In A Name?

Wisconsin is not the only name by which our state is recognized. Like many other states, Wisconsin has some nicknames, official or unofficial!

Badger State

America's Dairyland

Land of Lakes

State Capital:
Madison

Since 1836

The governing authority for the Wisconsin Territory met on July 3,1836 to choose a site for the capital. They decided to name the capital Madison, in honor of President James Madison. Building on the uninhabited site began in the winter of 1836. The current Wisconsin State Capitol was completed in 1917. Its dome is 300 feet (91 meters) high—almost as tall as the nation's Capitol in Washington, D.C.! The top of the dome features a sculpture of a woman called *Wisconsin*.

Word Definition

CAPITAL: a town or city that is the official seat of government
CAPITOL: the building in which the government officials meet

Who's in Charge Here?

Wisconsin's GOVERNMENT has three branches:

EXECUTIVE

The governor, lieutenant governor, secretary of state, treasurer, attorney general, and superintendent of public instruction

LEGISLATVE

The legislative branch is called the General Assembly.

Two Houses: The Senate (33 members) and the Assembly (99 members)

JUDICIAL

Seven justices, headed by supreme court justice, plus Court of Appeals, Circuit Courts, Municipal Courts

Wisconsin's state constitution was approved in 1848. It has had 132 amendments, but has never been rewritten. The forefathers of this state knew what they were doing when they wrote the first one!

State Flag

It's a Grand Old Flag!

The state flag of Wisconsin was adopted in 1913. The main feature of the flag is the state seal, which shows a badger and symbols for industry and agriculture. The flag is flown on many state, city, and town buildings.

State Seal & Motto

State Seal

The Great Seal of the State of Wisconsin features important symbols of the state, such as a badger, a cornucopia of fruit and vegetables, and a pyramid of pig lead.

State Seal & Motto

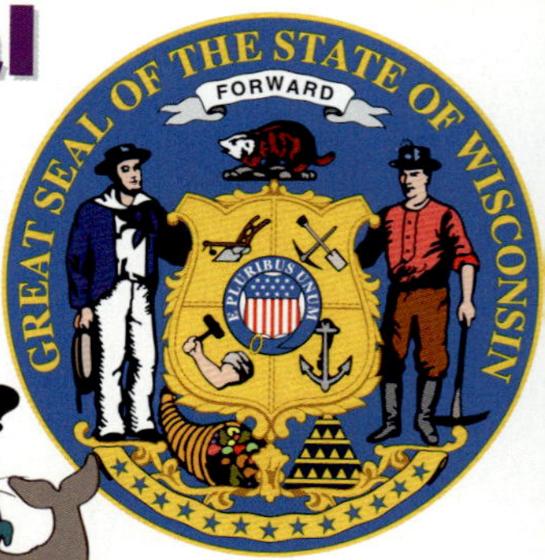

Word Definition

MOTTO: a sentence, phrase, or word expressing the spirit or purpose of an organization or group

State Motto

Wisconsin's state motto is... Forward

Wisconsin's state motto of "Forward" shows that it is a progressive state. The statue of the woman on top of the state capitol is sometimes called "Miss Forward."

State Tree & Bird

Sugar Maple

Wisconsin schoolchildren selected the Sugar Maple as their favorite tree not once, but twice—first in 1893 and again in 1948. In 1949, the state lawmakers took a cue from the kids and made it official.

Sugar Maples are popular because their sweet sap is the main ingredient in maple syrup and maple sugar. They are brilliant in the fall when their leaves turn yellow, orange, and deep red.

The Robin was chosen by Wisconsin's schoolchildren to be the state bird in 1927. It received twice as many votes as other birds!

Robin

The state bird of Wisconsin is the Robin. The Robin got its name from homesick European settlers who named it for a bird in their homeland that also has a red breast.

Wood Violet

...And purple all the ground with vernal flowers.—John Milton

What a choice! Wisconsin's schoolchildren nominated four flowers to be the state flower, including the wood violet, the wild rose, the trailing arbutus, and the white water lily. On Arbor Day, 1908, they voted and the Wood Violet was the winner. In 1949, the Wisconsin lawmakers made it official.

Violet hybrids occur frequently in nature. Hybrid flowers are cross-pollinated. Insects can easily pollinate the flowers because of their open petals.

State Animal

BADGER

Wisconsin's state animal, the Badger, appears on the state flag, state seal, and in the capitol architecture. It is even mentioned in the state song.

Badgers move about slowly and have a reputation for being aggressive if they're threatened. They are also like skunks and can protect themselves by spewing out a foul-smelling scent.

More State Animals

State Wildlife Animal: White-tailed Deer

More State Animals

The badger wasn't a hands-down winner in the state animal vote. People in northern Wisconsin wanted it to be the White-tailed Deer. To keep everyone happy, in 1957 it was named the state wildlife animal.

State Domesticated Animal: Dairy Cow

To recognize its importance to the state, Wisconsin added the "domesticated animal" category to its state symbols in 1971. The obvious choice was the Dairy Cow.

RIDDLE: What do you get when you cross the state animal with the state wildlife animal?

When you cross the state wildlife animal with the state domesticated animal?

Answer: A badgered white-tailed deer! A deer that produces cheese!

State Fossil, Mineral, & Rock

Trilobite

Trilobites lived underwater millions of years ago. Trilobite fossils are easy to find in Wisconsin. The Trilobite was named the state fossil in 1985.

GALENA

In 1971, Galena was named the state mineral. Galena is a major source of lead ore.

Red Granite

Red Granite, which is an igneous rock made of quartz and feldspar, is mined in several locations in Wisconsin. The feldspar is what gives the rock its red color. Red Granite is very hard and is used for buildings and monuments.

Add Milk!

While a number of states claim milk as their state beverage, Wisconsin can honestly claim it since it's the nation's leading dairy-producing state. Milk was named the state beverage in 1987.

Wisconsin dairy farmers owe part of their success to grass! A certain type of English grass that Wisconsin dairy farmers planted helped the cows produce large quantities of flavorful milk.

A University of Wisconsin professor, Stephen M. Babcock, helped the dairy industry when he invented a way to find out the butterfat content in milk. Butterfat determines how good cheese tastes. The more, the better!

American Water Spaniel

In 1985, the Wisconsin General Assembly named the American Water Spaniel as the state dog. This came about through the efforts of eighth-grade students at Washington Junior High School in New London.

The American Water Spaniel is one of only five dog breeds that are entirely native to the United States, and the only one native to Wisconsin. In 1920, the United Kennel Club recognized the American Water Spaniel.

While they're not considered "flashy" show dogs, American Water Spaniels are known for their versatility, intelligence, and good temperament. They are valued as hunters and watchdogs, and for their loyalty as family pets.

What It Takes to Feed the Cows

All those cows in Wisconsin that produce dairy products have to be fed. Farmers have to grow feed for cattle, and you can't grow crops without soil!

Antigo Silt Loam

In 1983, Antigo Silt Loam was designated the state soil. This special designation also reminds Wisconsinites of the responsibility they have to take for their land. Antigo Silt Loam didn't just happen overnight—it took 10,000 years to form.

Corn

Wisconsin is a major Corn producing state. Some of the Corn is used for people food, and some of it is used to fill up those cows. In 1989, Corn was declared the state grain.

State Insect

Honeybee

– Apis mellifera

Third-graders at Holy Family School in Marinette asked the General Assembly to adopt the Honeybee as the state insect. In 1977, the Honeybee was named the state insect.

Scientists have discovered that Honeybees do a special dance to let other bees know where and how far away flowers are.

Muskellunge

It took members of the Wisconsin legislature 14 years, but they were finally able to pass legislation naming the state fish the Muskellunge. The only competition for the Muskie was the trout. The Muskie was named the state fish in 1955.

If you're lucky enough to catch a Muskie, you're not likely to fry it up in a pan. Muskies are considered trophy fish to be mounted and displayed.

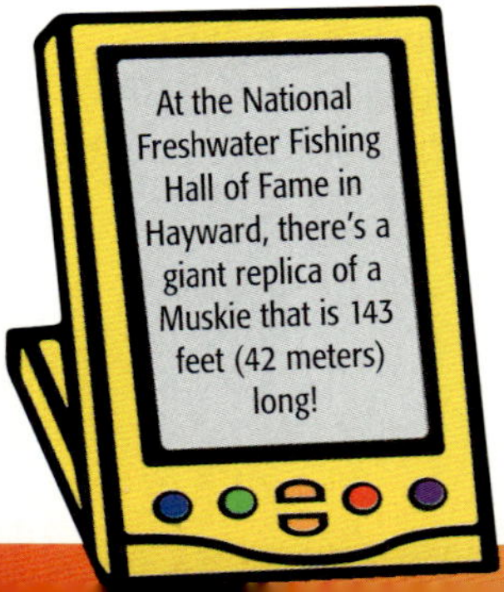

State Map

The State of Wisconsin

Most of Wisconsin was covered by glaciers four times in the last million years before the ice moved northward and plants and animals could make the region their home.

If all Wisconsin's lakes were combined, they would cover almost one million acres (400,000 hectares)!

State Location

Wisconsin is located in the northern central portion of the United States, not very far from Canada.

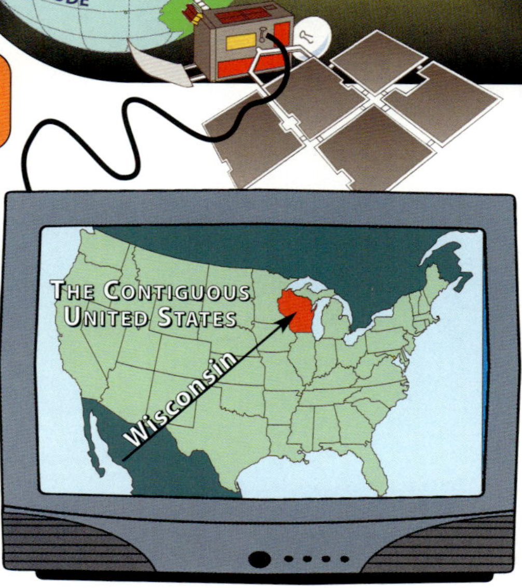

Word Definition

LATITUDE: Imaginary lines which run horizontally east and west around the globe
LONGITUDE: Imaginary lines which run vertically north and south around the globe

UP, DOWN, AROUND!

These border Wisconsin:

States: Michigan, Minnesota, Iowa, Illinois

Bodies of water: Lake Superior, Lake Michigan

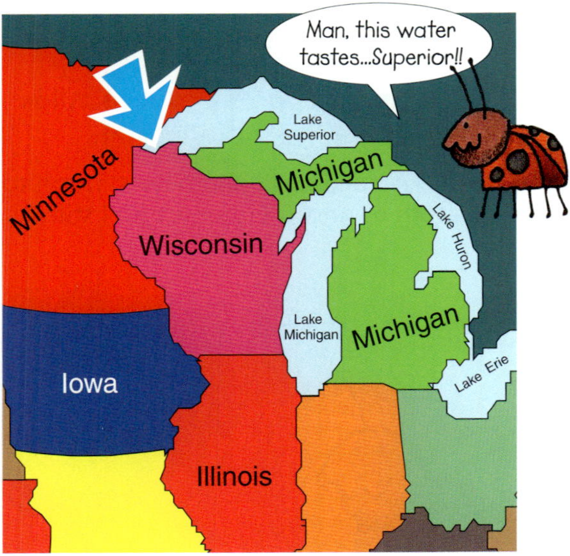

I'll Take the High Road...

Wisconsin is 295 miles (472 kilometers) east to west...or west to east. Either way, it's a long drive!

Total Area: Approx. 65,500 square miles (170,300 square kilometers)

Land Area: Approx. 54,314 square miles (141,216 square kilometers)

Wisconsin is 320 miles (512 kilometers) north to south...or south to north. Either way, it's still a long drive.

First There's Highs, Then There's Lows

Highest Point

Timms Hill — 1,952 feet (595 meters) above sea level

A sawmill on Timms Hill closed in 1907. The unused logs sank to the bottom of Bass Lake. In 1925 timber operations began again. The logs were brought up from the bottom of the lake, and they were sound enough to be sawed into lumber!

Lowest Point

581 feet (177 meters) above sea level along Lake Michigan

I'm County-ing on You!

Wisconsin is divided into 72 counties.

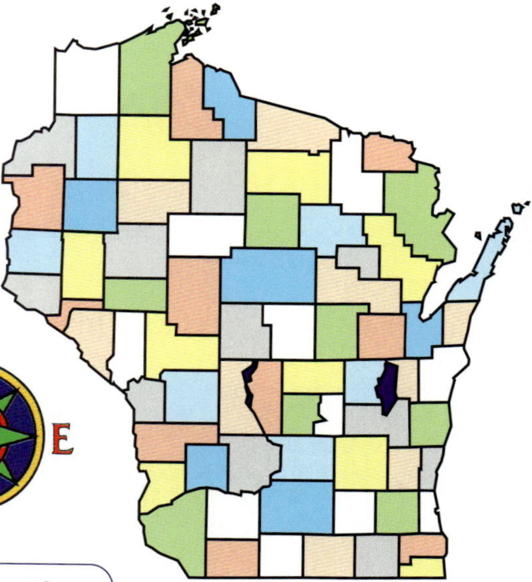

Word
Definition

COUNTY:
an administrative subdivision of a state or territory

Natural Resources

Word Definition

NATURAL RESOURCES: things that exist in or are formed by nature

Minerals:

Galena

Iron

Zinc-sulfide

Copper

Lime

Weather, Or Not?!

Windstorms move across Wisconsin quickly since there are no high mountains to slow them down. Generally, the summers are warm. There is little humidity. The winters are long and cold. Many small lakes and streams freeze in December and don't thaw out until April!

Highest temperature: 114°F (46°C), Wisconsin Dells, July 1936

°F=Degrees Fahrenheit °C=Degrees Celsius

Lowest temperature: -54°F (-47°C), Danbury, January 1922

Lake Michigan and Lake Superior affect the temperature of the coast and cause it to be very different from areas just a few miles inland.

Back On Top

Wisconsin's land has been described as being "a little bit of everything that makes a land livable." Today, there aren't any extreme land formations—no high mountains or deserts. Most of the land can be described as being a plain.

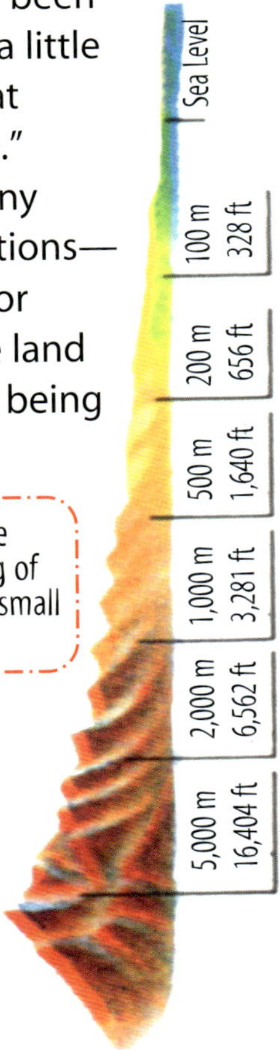

Word Definition

TOPOGRAPHY: the detailed mapping of the features of a small area or district

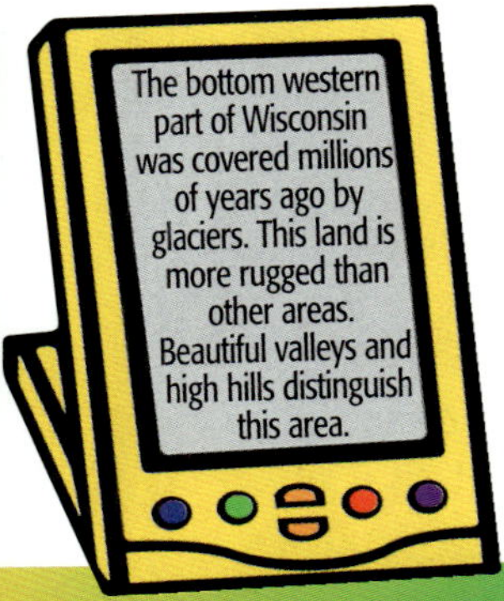

Glacial Effects

As prehistoric glaciers moved out of the Wisconsin area, falling rocks created mounds. These mounds are called kames. There are also long mounds called drumlins. Round craters formed by the glaciers that filled with water and became ponds are called kettles. As more glacial ice melted and formed rivers, they deposited sand and gravel. These deposits are known as eskers.

Rib Mountain is located near the center of the state. It is a single mountain of rock that was forced up out of the earth's crust thousands of years ago.

Down by the River

Wisconsin has hundreds of waterfalls. Big Manitou Falls at Pattison State Park is the highest. It is 165 feet (49.5 meters) high. If Wisconsin's 144 canoe rivers were all joined end to end, they would make a 3,484-mile (5,609 kilometers) canoe ride!

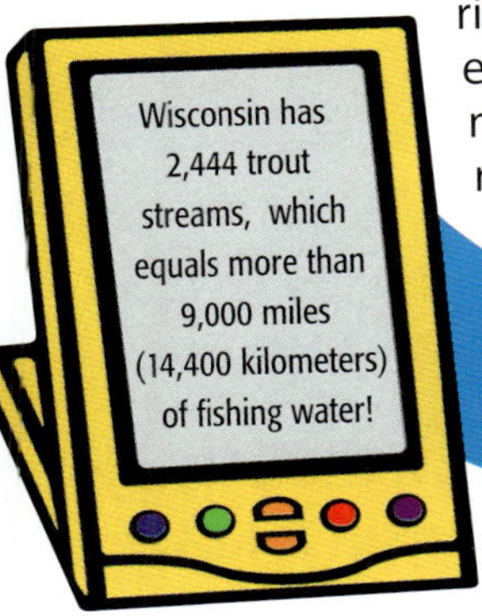

Here are some of Wisconsin's major rivers:

- **Mississippi**
- **Wisconsin**
- **Chippewa**
- **Black**
- **Fox**
- **Menominee**
- **Peshtigo**
- **St. Croix**
- **Rock**

Land of Lakes

Wisconsin earned its nickname of Land of Lakes. It has more than 15,000 lakes!

Here's a list of major Wisconsin lakes:

- **Lake Winnebago** is the largest
- **Big Green Lake** is the deepest
- **Lake Pepin**
- **Lake Poygan**
- **Lake Koshkonong**
- **Lake Geneva**

The capital city of Madison is one of America's prettiest smaller cities because it is surrounded by the beautiful lakes, Mendota, Monona, Waubesa, and Kegonsa.

ARE YOU A CITY MOUSE... OR COUNTRY MOUSE?

Have you heard of these wonderful Wisconsin city, town, and crossroad names? Perhaps you can start your own collection!

LARGER TOWNS:

Milwaukee
Madison
Green Bay
Racine
Kenosha
Appleton
West Allis
Waukesha
Eau Claire

SMALLER TOWNS:

Bloomer
Brown Deer
Butternut
Embarrass
Endeavor
Friendship
Friesville
Hazel Green
Loyal
Luck
Pound

Transportation

Major Interstate Highways

I-53, I-63, I-94, I-90, I-51, I-41, I-43
Wisconsin has about 108,000 miles (172,800 kilometers) of paved highways.

Railroads

There are about 5,000 miles (about 8,000 kilometers) of railroad tracks in Wisconsin.

Airports

Mitchell Field in Milwaukee is the state's busiest airport, but there are more than 400 airports in Wisconsin!

Ports

Wisconsin has 50 harbors on Lake Michigan, Lake Superior, and the Mississippi River.

Timeline

12,000BC	Last glaciers retreat north across Wisconsin
300BC–AD500	Hopewell burial mounds built
800–1600s	Fox, Sauk, Winnebago people occupy area
1634	Jean Nicolet becomes first European in the area
1718	French build Green Bay fort
1763	British defeat French; Wisconsin becomes part of British territory under Treaty of Paris
1783	Wisconsin becomes part of U.S. under Second Treaty of Paris
1816	John Jacob Astor's American Fur Company founded
1825	Erie Canal opens, easing migration to the West
1836	Territory of Wisconsin created
1848	Wisconsin becomes the thirtieth state
1917	Wisconsin is first state to identify highways by number
1947	First Wisconsin television station, WTMJ-TV, begins broadcasting from Milwaukee
1959	St. Lawrence Seaway opens
1967	Civil-rights demonstrators march for open-housing ordinance in Milwaukee
1976	U.S. District Court orders integration of Milwaukee schools
1996	Wisconsin Works program is enacted
2001	On to the 21st century!

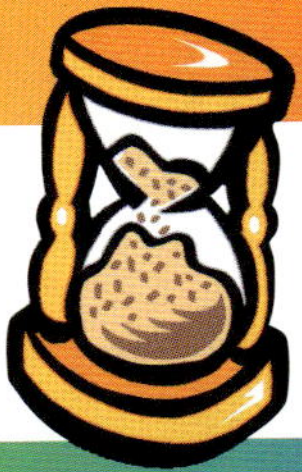

Here come the humans!

Thousands of years ago, ancient peoples inhabited Wisconsin. They may have originally come across a frozen bridge of land between Asia and Alaska. If so, they slowly traveled east until some settled in what would one day become the state of Wisconsin.

About 3000 BC they learned to make ax heads and spear points from copper.

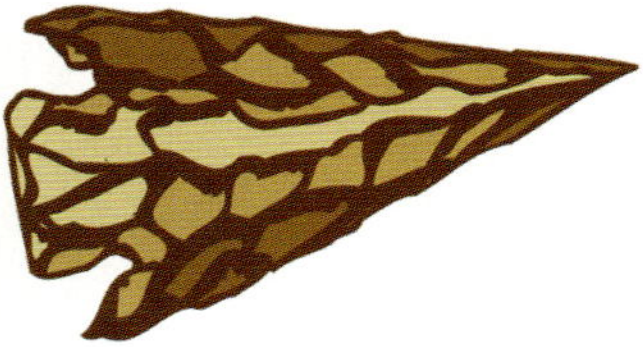

Native Americans Once Ruled!

Between 500 and 1300, Wisconsin Indians built large earthen structures we call mounds. Many of these structures still stand today. They can be shaped like pyramids, people, or animals. These mounds may have been built for ceremonial or religious purposes.

Word Definition

WAMPUM: beads, pierced and strung, used by Indians as money, or for ornaments or ceremonies.

Land Ho!

The first Europeans to reach Wisconsin traveled through the Great Lakes by canoe. They came ashore at the present day city of Green Bay. These explorers searched for a route through North America to the Pacific Ocean. Although they never found a sea route to the Pacific, they did claim the newly discovered land for France.

Voyageurs (French trappers and traders) traveled throughout Wisconsin. They sold many furs to the Old World and explored much of the area.

Home, Sweet Home

Roman Catholic priests established the first missions in Wisconsin. These missions were built to convert the Native Americans to Christianity. These missions helped establish relationships between the French and Native Americans.

You can visit one of the missions established by Father Claude Allouez in De Pere.

Fertile Farms

One of Wisconsin's most important crops is corn. Wisconsin belongs to a group of states called the corn belt. Some of the corn grown in Wisconsin is used to feed the many cows in the state. Sometimes corn on the cob, or corn bread ends up on the dinner plate.

Fact Or Fiction?

Paul Bunyan is a Wisconsin legend. The legend says that Paul was a lumberjack, and he was very big. After walking through Wisconsin, his footprints became the many thousands of lakes found in the northern part of the state. He also had a large friend named Babe. Babe was a giant blue ox who was twice as big as all outdoors.

Freedom!

Some settlers in the New World felt that England ignored their ideas and concerns. In 1775, the colonies went to war with England. On July 4th, 1776, the Declaration of Independence was signed. At the time of the American Revolution, there were only a small number of Europeans living in Wisconsin. Many of them were fur traders who may not have known much about the war. The British soldiers stationed in the area kept control of Wisconsin until the War of 1812.

Of Human Bondage

Slavery existed in Wisconsin as far back as French colonial days, but at that time, there were very few slaves in the area. The Northwest Ordinance issued by the United States outlawed bringing new slaves into the territory, but did not free slaves already living in Wisconsin. Henry Dodge, Wisconsin's first territorial governor, owned slaves until 1838. The issue of slavery and states' rights led to the Civil War. In 1865, the 13th amendment abolished slavery in the United States.

Brother

The Civil War was fought between the American states. The argument was over the right of the states to make their own decisions, including whether or not to own slaves. Some of the Southern states began to secede (leave) the Union.

Word Definition

BRIGADE: a unit of the U.S. Army made up of more than one battalion.

vs. Brother

They formed the Confederate States of America. Wisconsin remained loyal to the United States. Many brave soldiers from Wisconsin fought in a group called the Iron Brigade.

Get It In Writing!

Declaration of Independence,
1776

Northwest Ordinance,
1787

U.S. Constitution,
1789

State Constitution,
1848

State Income Tax,
1911

Unemployment Insurance Law,
1932

WELCOME TO AMERICA!

Wisconsinites have come to Wisconsin from other states and many other countries on almost every continent! As time has gone by, Wisconsin's population has grown more diverse. This means that people of different races and from different cultures and ethnic backgrounds have moved to Wisconsin.

In the past, many immigrants have come to Wisconsin from Germany, England, Ireland, Scotland, Sweden, Denmark, Finland, and Norway. Slaves immigrated (involuntarily) from Africa. In 1852, Wisconsin established an office in New York City to attract immigrants to the state. More recently, people have migrated to Wisconsin from Hispanic countries such as Mexico. Many immigrants eventually become U.S. citizens.

Disasters & Catastrophes!

1871

Twelve hundred people killed in Peshtigo forest fire–900 more than in the Great Chicago Fire!

1970

University of Wisconsin bombed; one person killed

1975

Edmund Fitzgerald sinks during a violent storm on Lake Superior; 29 sailors dead

1986

Violent rainstorm causes flooding, two people killed, 10,000 homes flooded, and $27 million in property damage

Legal Stuff

1905

State civil service law established

1911

Wisconsin passes first state income tax law

1932

Law to compensate workers for unemployment passes—First in nation!

Legal Stuff

1961

Wisconsin passes safety belt law; first seat belt law in the nation—Buckle up, Wisconsin!

1972

Legal voting age lowered from 21 to 18

1973

Menominee tribe regains federal recognition

1856

First kindergarten established by Margarethe Meyer Schurz at Watertown

1875

Women allowed to vote for school offices

1919

Wisconsin becomes first state to register ratification of the 19th Amendment, which gives women the right to vote!

1960

Dena Smith becomes first woman elected to a statewide office as state treasurer

Fight!, Fight!, Fight!

- French and Indian War
- Revolutionary War
- War of 1812
- Black Hawk War
- Civil War
- Spanish-American War
- World War I
- World War II
- Korean War
- Vietnam War
- Persian Gulf War

America's Dairyland

Wisconsin is known as America's Dairyland. Cows are raised to provide milk for you and me. Milk is used to make cheese, yogurt, butter, and ice cream.

Wisconsin leads the nation in cheese production. The center of cheesemaking in the state is Monroe County. Because of the cheese industry, Wisconsinites have the humorous nickname "Cheeseheads." Green Bay Packer fans take pride in this nickname by wearing "cheesehead hats" to football games.

Wisconsinites eat nearly 21 million gallons of ice cream every year. The very first ice cream sundae was "scooped" in 1881 in Two Rivers. Was it two scoops in Two Rivers, or maybe three?

In 1881, Edward Berner, of Two Rivers, came up with a dessert when he poured chocolate syrup over Wisconsin ice cream. He would only sell his "sundaes" on Sunday.

Indian Tribes

- Chippewa (Ojibwa)
- Menominee
- Oneida
- Potawatomi
- Ho-Chunk (Winnebago)
- Iroquois
- Ottawa
- Huron
- Miami
- Fox
- Dakota Sioux (Santee)

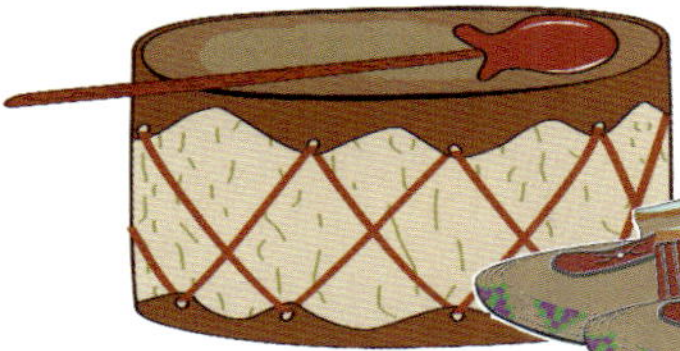

Indian mounds in the shape of animals are called effigy mounds and stand about 36 inches (90 centimeters) tall. More effigy mounds were built in Wisconsin than any other state.

Early Wisconsin Indians hunted, farmed the land, and harvested wild rice from the Great Lakes area. Children played games such as Hide and Seek and Follow My Leader. They told time by the full moons of the harvest season, and lived in lodges that were made from saplings covered with bark.

The Indians of Wisconsin could not have known that the coming of the settlers would mean an end to their way of life they had known for hundreds of years!

Here, There, Everywhere!

In 1634, while trying to find a route to the Pacific Ocean, French explorer, *Jean Nicolet*, became the first known European to enter Lake Michigan. He sailed from eastern Canada and landed on the shores of Green Bay. He thought he had landed in China.

In 1660, a Roman Catholic priest, *René Ménard*, established a mission on the Chippewa River.

About 1665, *Father Claude Allouez* established several missions, including one near present-day De Pere.

Father Jacques Marquette and *Louis Jolliet* sailed into Green Bay and into the Fox River.

John Muir, from Scotland, was a naturalist and explorer who lived in Marquette County. He helped establish the Sierra Club and America's national park system.

Roy Chapman Andrews was an explorer from Wisconsin who found the first dinosaur egg in Asia's Gobi Desert.

Founding Fathers

PIERRE ESPRIT RADISSON, of Canada, built the first settler's house, a log cabin, on the site of the present-day city of Green Bay.

CHARLES DE LANGLADE built the first farm in the Green Bay area. He was the most well-known fur trader and later called the "father of Wisconsin."

OSHKOSH was a Menominee Indian who led the successful effort to keep his tribal lands in Wisconsin for his people.

SOLOMON JUNEAU was a trader and early Milwaukee resident.

SAMUEL C. MAZZUCHELLI was a community leader and missionary.

JOHN JACOB ASTOR secured the Upper Mississippi fur trade from the British and French by using his influence in Washington, D.C.

Voyageur JACOB ROI, a French trapper, built a cottage at La Baye (Green Bay) in 1776. It is Green Bay's oldest home.

Founding Mothers

LILLIE ROSA MINOKA, of Mohawk descent, became a doctor and ministered to the Oneidas. She was adopted by the Oneida tribe. They called her "She Who Serves."

ADA JAMES was an outspoken advocate of women's rights. Ada and her father, David, worked for suffrage and equal rights.

FRANCES WILLARD was a famous suffragist and campaigner for the Women's Christian Temperance Union. The United States Congress named her the "first woman of the 19th century."

CARRIE CHAPMAN CATT was a suffragist who worked hard for equal rights for women. She reorganized the League of Women Voters after passage of the 19th Amendment gave women the right to vote.

Famous Native-Americans

BLACK HAWK was a Sauk Indian leader who attempted to restore his tribe's homeland in Illinois. He and his people battled the U.S. militia unsuccessfully in Illinois and Wisconsin. All but a few were slaughtered. The few that survived were captured by the militia or other Indian tribes.

ADA DEER was born in 1935 on the Menominee Indian Reservation. She studied at UW-Madison and became the first Menominee to receive a degree. Ada became a spokesperson for DRUMS (Determination of Rights and Unity for Menominee Shareholders). In 1954, the Menominee voted to become their own county, but suffered financial hardship after federal support was terminated. Ada worked hard to restore reservation status for her people, and in 1973, the Menominee Restoration Act was signed into law.

Potawatomi CHIEF KAHQUADOS was an expert lumberjack and self-taught surveyor who lived in the forests of northern Door County. He tried to improve the lives of his people. He made many trips to Washington, D.C. to deliver proposals to the Bureau of Indian Affairs.

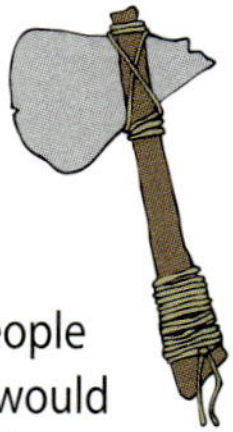

Chief RED BIRD was a Winnebago, or Ho-Chunk, chief who fought bravely against settlers who came to Wisconsin to mine lead near Mineral Point.

YELLOW THUNDER led the Winnebago, or Ho-Chunk, people to purchase plots of land in Wisconsin so that they would not be forced by the U.S. government to leave their homes.

SEND IN THE CLOWNS!

Have you ever been to a circus? You have? Well then, chances are you've seen a Ringling Brothers show. The five Ringling brothers, Albert, Charles, Alfred, Otto, and John, held the very first show in 1884 in their hometown of Baraboo. The star performers included a billy goat, rabbits, chickens, and Zachary the horse.

Over the next 20 years, the big top business grew and grew! The Ringlings bought the Barnum & Bailey Circus in 1906. The family business was now the Ringling Brothers and Barnum & Bailey Circus—the "Greatest Show on Earth!"

The city of Delavan is also known as a city that clowns around. The Clown Hall of Fame was established in 1987 to honor the entertainers who delight children of all ages! In 1989, Red Skelton, Otto Greibling, Emmett Kelly, Sr., Mark Anthony, Felix Adler, and Lou Jacobs were the first six funny men to be inducted. In 1992, Gene "Cousin Otto" Lee of Milwaukee became the first clown from Wisconsin to be inducted into the Hall of Fame.

FAMOUS WISCONSIN SPORTS FIGURES:

MARY JEAN MALOTTE–won world championship birling contest; paid her way through college with her winnings

EARL L. "CURLY" LAMBEAU–professional football coach, founded and coached the Green Bay Packers, helped create National Football League

VINCE LOMBARDI–professional football coach, coached the Green Bay Packers, first to win three consecutive NFL championships

WALTER W. "RED" SMITH–sports columnist and commentator, received Pulitzer Prize

ALLAN "BUD" SELIG–owner of the American League Milwaukee Brewers professional baseball team

HANK AARON–homerun king who played with the National League Braves while they were in Milwaukee from 1953 to 1966

KAREEM ABDUL-JABBAR–professional basketball player who played with Milwaukee Bucks

ERIC HEIDEN–Olympic speed skater, won five gold medals at the 1980 Winter Olympics

DAN JANSEN–speed skater who set a world record at the 1994 Winter Olympics

Entertainers

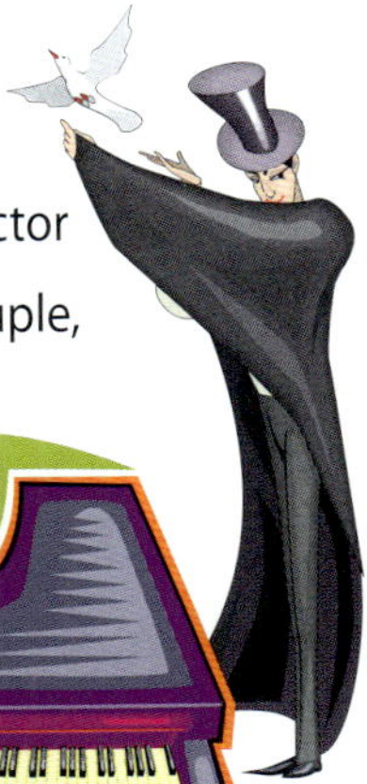

HARRY HOUDINI–world famous magician and escape artist

DON AMECHE–Academy Award-winning actor

LYNN FONTAINE and ALFRED LUNT–acting couple, awarded Presidential Medal of Freedom in 1964

LIBERACE–pianist and singer

FREDERIC MARCH–Academy award winning actor

SPENCER TRACY–Academy award-winning actor

ORSON WELLS–actor and director

GENE WILDER–actor, starred in *Willy Wonka and the Chocolate Factory*

GARY BURGHOFF–played Radar O'Reilly on television show, *MASH*

WOODY HERMAN–jazz musician

CARRIE JACOBS BOND–songwriter

RIDDLE: What was the name of the little boy who won the contest and inherited the Wonka candy factory?

Answer: Charlie

Authors

- AUGUST DERLETH–author
- EDNA FERBER–author, received Pulitzer Prize for *So Big*
- ZONA GALE–author, received Pulitzer Prize for *Miss Lulu Bett*
- HAMLIN GARLAND–author, received Pulitzer Prize for *A Daughter of the Middle Border*
- LORINE NIEDECKER–poet
- LAURA INGALLS WILDER–author of children's books, wrote a series of books based on her life in the Midwest
- ALDO LEOPOLD–teacher, author, environmentalist
- THORNTON WILDER–author, received Pulitzer Prize for *The Bridge of San Luis Rey* and plays, *Our Town* and *The Skin of Our Teeth*
- THORSTEIN VEBLEN–economist and author, wrote *The Theory of the Leisure Class*
- OLYMPIA BROWN–minister and publisher

????????

Which famous author wrote *Little House on the Prairie*?

ANSWER: Laura Ingalls Wilder

Artists

GEORGIA O'KEEFFE– painter of flowers and landscapes, awarded Presidential Medal of Freedom

HELEN FARNSWORTH MEARS– sculptor who created the Frances Willard statue in the U.S. Capitol and *The Genius of Wisconsin* on display at the capitol building in Madison

EDWIN HOWLAND BLASHFIELD–painter, created the murals at the capitol building in Madison

VINNIE REAM–sculptor

AARON BOHROD– painter, won Guggenheim Fellowships

OWEN J. GROMME– wildlife artist, painter

JULIETTE KINZIE–artist and writer

RICHARD LIPPOLD–artist, sculptor

FRED SMITH–folk artist called the "Picasso of the Northwoods"

Very Important People

Michael Red Cloud, Jr.–soldier, Korean War hero, awarded Medal of Honor posthumously for bravery in Korea

Margarethe Meyer Schurz–opened first U.S. kindergarten in Watertown

John T. Appleby–patented the knotter which ties bundles of grain with twine

Stephen W. Babcock–chemist, invented a way to measure the amount of butterfat in milk

Mary Baker Eddy–founder of the Church of Christ Scientist

William Horlick–created Malted Milk

John Bardeen–physicist, won Nobel Prize for developing the transistor and for the theory of superconductivity

More VIPs

Dr. William Beaumont–Army surgeon

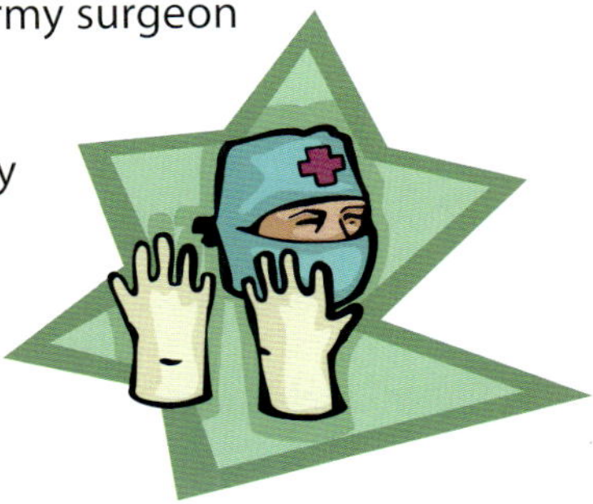

John Bascom–educator, president of the University of Wisconsin

Richard Ira "Dick" Bong–aviator, World War II pilot, awarded Medal of Honor

Frank Lloyd Wright–architect

Walter Annenberg–media tycoon

Jim Lovell–astronaut

King Camp Gillette–industrialist

Increase A. Lapham–father of the Weather Service

Hercules L. Dousman–business leader

Ole Evinrude–invented first outboard motor for mass production

Frederick Jackson Turner–historian, received Pulitzer Prize for history

Good Guys & Gals

Golda Meir was born in 1898 in the Ukraine. She and her family emigrated to Milwaukee to escape Anti-Semitism (hatred of Jews) in her homeland. She later moved to Israel, served in the Knesset, and was elected prime minister of Israel.

Brooks Stevens designed many notable automobiles, trains, motorcycles, appliances and helped found the Industrial Designers Society of America.

Father James Edward Groppi was a Catholic Priest and civil rights activist.

Harry Steenbock was a biochemist who produced Vitamin D using ultraviolet light.

Charles Van Hise was president of the University of Wisconsin. He expanded the university into many new fields and doubled university enrollment.

Mildred Fish Harnach organized resistance groups and sent intelligence information to the Allies during World War II.

Cordelia Harvey established military hospitals in the North during the Civil War.

Mary Lasker was a philanthropist whose financial donations supported cancer research. She was awarded the Presidential Medal of Freedom.

Laura Ross Wolcott was the first woman physician in Wisconsin and first president of the Wisconsin Woman's Suffrage Association.

A Very Bad Guy:

Al Capone was a notorious criminal in the 1920s. Couderay was his Northwoods hideout. On the grounds were a machine-gun tower, a fieldstone lodge, and Cranberry Lake. Some say some of Capone's enemies ended up wearing "cement shoes" in Cranberry Lake.

Political Leaders

Robert M. La Follette, Sr.–political leader, progressive reformer, governor, U.S. Senator

Belle Case La Follette–lawyer, editor, fought for women's rights

Carl Schurz–German immigrant, brigadier general in the Union Army, U.S. Secretary of the Interior

Vel Phillips–first woman and first African-American elected to Milwaukee's city council

Dena Smith–state treasurer, first woman elected to a major state office

Henry Dodge–politician, soldier, and miner

James Duane Doty–politician and land speculator

William Vilas–politician, U.S. Postmaster General

Cadwallader C. Washburn–businessman, congressman, governor

William Dempster Hoard–farmer and governor

Walter J. Kohler, Sr.–industrialist and governor

Kathryn Morrison–senator

Shirley S. Abrahamson–state supreme court justice

William H. Rehnquist–U.S. supreme court justice

Joe McCarthy–controversial U.S. senator

Keeping the Faith

Catholic bark chapel, Green Bay—part of Heritage Hill State Park; used by early Jesuit missionaries

First Congregational Church, Beloit—part of the Hanchett-Bartlett Homestead; built by noted area architect Lucas Bradley in 1859

Saint Josaphat Basilica, Milwaukee—first Polish basilica in North America; Neo-Renaissance structure, designed in 1897 by Erhard Brielmaier

Church of the Gesu, Milwaukee—located on the Marquette University campus; boasts towering French Gothic spires and an exceptional pipe organ

SCHOOLS

Some of Wisconsin's colleges and universities:

Milton College, Milton; first institution of higher education in the state

University of Wisconsin, Madison

The first statewide vocational and adult-educational network in the U.S. was established in Wisconsin in 1911.

Marquette University, Milwaukee

Mount Mary College, Milwaukee

Lawrence University, Appleton

Beloit College, Beloit

Ripon College, Ripon

Carroll College, Waukesha; oldest college in the state

Some of Wisconsin's historical sites include:

- **Old World Wisconsin**
- **White Pillars**
- **Potawatomi Lighthouse**
- **Pinecrest Historical Village**
- **Little White Schoolhouse**
- **Pendarvis**

Some of Wisconsin's parks include:

- **Peninsula State Park, Green Bay**
- **Potawatomi State Park, Sturgeon Bay**
- **Pattison State Park,** features Big Manitou Falls
- **Interstate Park,** oldest of Wisconsin's state parks; noted for its river gorge and rocky bluffs
- **Kohler-Andrae State Park,** near Sheboygan; includes a wide sandy beach on Lake Michigan

The state Historical Society of Wisconsin is the oldest state historical society in the nation.

Early Residency

Tank Cottage, Green Bay; one of the oldest houses existing in the state

Milton House, Milton; poured concrete building constructed on a hexagonal plan; served as a stagecoach stop and as a station on the Underground Railroad

Old Wade House, near Sheboygan

Pabst Mansion, Milwaukee; built in 1893 and contains 37 rooms

Erie Street Cottages, Racine

Villa Louis, Prairie du Chien

Old Executive Mansion, Madison; governor's residence from 1883–1950

Blue Mounds and Little Norway, Mount Horeb; early Norwegian settlements

Swiss Historical Village, New Glarus

Octagon House, Watertown

Taliesin, Spring Green; built in 1911 by famed architect Frank Lloyd Wright

Forts and Battles

Some of Wisconsin's Forts

- *Fort Winnebago, Portage*
- *Fort Howard, near Green Bay*
- *Fort Crawford, Prairie du Chien*

Some of Wisconsin's Battles

Black Hawk War

Two battles between the Sauk Indians and a U.S. militia occurred in 1832. Chief Black Hawk and 1,000 men, women, and children of the Sauk tribe tried to peacefully return to their old land in Illinois to hunt and grow corn. They were not allowed back and tried to return to Wisconsin. Upon hearing of Black Hawk's flight back into Wisconsin, frontier fighter Colonel Henry Dodge and his troops (including young Abe Lincoln) pursued the retreating Indians.

The Battle of Wisconsin Heights occurred just southeast of Sauk City on July 21, 1832. The women and children escaped across the river. The warriors stood their ground until nightfall, then fled.

The Battle of Bad Axe occurred on August 2, 1832 near present-day De Soto, where the Bad Axe River flows into the Mississippi. Almost all of Black Hawk's followers were massacred. He was taken as prisoner.

Libraries

Check out the following special state libraries! (Do you have a library card? Have you worn it out yet?!)

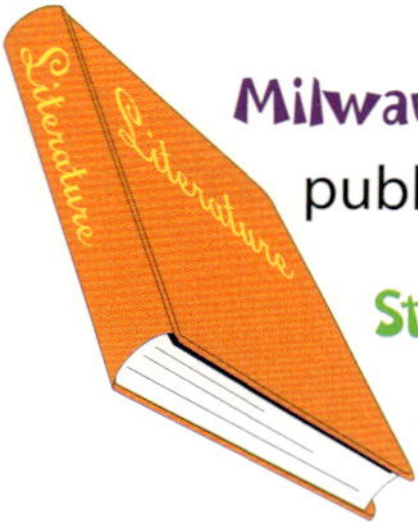

Milwaukee Public Library–leading public library in the state

State Historical Society Library, Madison–contains extensive collections on state history

University of Wisconsin Library, Madison

Legislative Reference Library, Madison–provides research services for state legislators and helps them in the drafting of legislation

Zoos & Attractions

National Fresh Water Fishing Hall of Fame, Hayward

Green Bay Packer Hall of Fame, Green Bay

Mitchell Park, Milwaukee

Noah's Ark, Wisconsin Dells–home to the nation's largest water-theme park

Wolfway Farm, West Salem–working dairy farm on 560 acres (224 hectares)

Granton Cheese Factory, Granton–Genuine Amish cheese and gifts

Vacationland Farm, Sister Bay

Milwaukee County Zoo, Milwaukee

Henry Vilas Park Zoo, Madison

Lincoln Park Zoo, Manitowoc

Museums

- **Madeline Island Historical Museum**, Madeline Island
- **National Railroad Museum**, Green Bay
- **Wisconsin Maritime Museum**, Manitowoc
- **State Historical Museum**, Madison
- **Circus World Museum**, Baraboo
- **Milwaukee Public Museum**, Milwaukee
- **Door County Historical Museum**, Door Peninsula
- **Pinecrest Historical Village**, Manitowoc
- **Hoard Historical Museum and Dairy Shrine**, Fort Atkinson
- **Rhinelander Logging Museum**, Rhinelander
- **Painted Forest Folk Art Museum**, Baraboo
- **Clown Hall of Fame**, Milwaukee
- **Chippewa Valley Museum**, Eau Claire
- **Fairlawn Mansion and Museum**, Superior

Camp Randall Memorial Park,
Madison
–contains numerous statues, plaques, and markers commemorating the Civil War camp.

Memorials

Caddie Woodlawn Memorial Park,
Menomonie
–named for the 1935 Newbery Medal-winning children's book *Caddie Woodlawn* written by Carol Ryrie Brink.

The Arts

Pabst Theater, Milwaukee–built in 1895 for German-born beer tycoon, Frederick Pabst. The Victorian Baroque theater is known for its great acoustics.

Villa Terrace Decorative Arts Museum, Milwaukee–a 1922 villa that houses the Milwaukee Art Museum collection of decorative arts, period furnishings, and porcelain.

John Michael Kohler Art Center, Sheboygan–more than 30 folk art architectural sites catalogued in an effort to preserve them.

Bradley Sculpture Garden, River Hills–includes 61 sculptured pieces in the garden, created by great sculptors.

LAKESHORES

Wisconsin has lakeshores on both Lake Michigan and Lake Superior. An 11-mile (18-kilometer) stretch of lakeshore on the Bayfield Peninsula in Lake Superior is designated a national lakeshore. It also includes 21 of the 22 Apostle Islands.

LIGHTHOUSES

The Apostle Islands, on Lake Superior, are home to six 19th-century lighthouses. Keeping watch over Lake Michigan is the Cana Island Lighthouse, built in 1869.

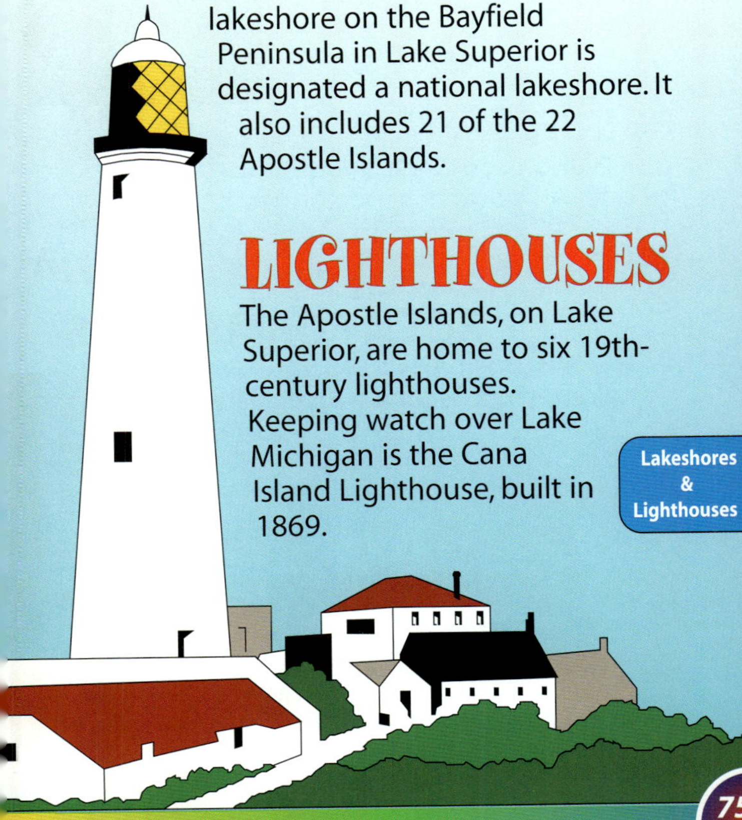

ROADS

- Kettle Moraine Scenic Drive
- Wisconsin River Scenic Drive
- Great River Road
- Scenic Route 13 of Lake Superior's southern shore

BRIDGES

York Island used to be two islands, but today it's one! A bridge of sand connects the two.

ROCK FORMATIONS

The Wisconsin Dells are unusual rocky cliffs along the Wisconsin River. The sandstone cliffs, deep water, and strange rock formations stretch for 17 miles (27 kilometers) along the river.

SWAMPS

Originally, the central part of the state was a large swamp. Once settlers arrived, the swamp was drained and filled for farmland. Horicon Marsh, near Waupun, is a 50-square-mile (129-square-kilometers) basin that filled in with water as a glacier retreated. This marsh attracts many migrating Canada geese.

CAVES

The Apostle Islands National Lakeshore has many interesting and mysterious limestone caves. There are over 300 known caves in Wisconsin.

KETTLES

Kettles are depressions caused by buried blocks of glacier ice that later melted and formed round ponds.

Animals of Wisconsin

Wisconsin's animals include:

Badger
Beaver
Black Bear
Coyote
Elk
Fox
Mink

Muskrat
Opossum
Porcupine
Raccoon
Snowshoe Hare
Squirrel
White-tailed Deer

Some of Wisconsin's endangered animals are:

Barn Owl
Canada Lynx
Northern Blue Butterfly
Ornate Box Turtle
Peregrine Falcon
Pine Marten
Queen Snake
Timber Wolf

Animals once living in Wisconsin, but no longer present:

Buffalo
Caribou
Trumpeter Swan
Wolverine

You may spy these birds in Wisconsin:

- Belted Kingfisher
- Black-capped Chickadee
- Blue Jay
- Bobwhite
- Cardinal
- Common Loon
- Crow
- Goldfinch
- Great Horned Owl
- Horned Lark
- Mallard
- Mockingbird
- Red-headed Woodpecker
- Red-tailed Hawk
- Ring-necked Pheasant
- Robin
- Rock Dove

Don't let these Wisconsin bugs bug you!

- Ant
- Beetle
- Bumblebee
- Butterfly
- Cicada
- Cricket
- Earwig
- Firefly
- Honeybee
- Katydid
- Lacewing
- Ladybug
- Luna Moth
- Mosquito
- Scorpionfly
- Stink Bug
- Yellow Jacket

Male cicadas can be heard loudly at the end of a summer day. They make their sounds with organs, called tymbals, in their abdomens.

Fish

Swimming in Wisconsin waters:

- Bass
- Bullhead
- Catfish
- Crappie
- Herring
- Lake Trout
- Muskellunge (Muskie)
- Northern Pike
- Perch
- Walleye
- Whitefish

Pond Critters

In Wisconsin's ponds, you may find:

- Bullfrog
- Crayfish
- Eel
- Leech
- Muskrat
- Mussels
- Newt
- Snails
- Toad
- Turtle
- Water Bug
- Water Snake
- Water Spider
- Whirligig Beetle

Whirligig beetles have two pairs of eyes–one pair looks above the water,the other looks under it.

The 22 Apostles

Lake Superior is home to the Apostle Islands. The islands were formed by the last Ice Age and consist of unique rock formations, caves, and rose-colored cliffs. European explorers counted only 12 islands, and decided to name them "the Apostles." There are actually 22 islands! In 1970, 21 of the islands and an 11-mile (18-kilometer) stretch of the Bayfield Peninsula shoreline was designated a National Lakeshore. Madeline Island, the largest and only commercial island, is not included on the National Lakeshore.

TREEMENDOUS!

THESE TREES GRACE THE STATE OF WISCONSIN:

Ash
Aspen
Basswood
Birch
Hawthorn
Hemlock
Maple
Oak
Pine
Spruce

Wild for Wisconsin Wildflowers!

- Black-eyed Susan
- Buttercup
- Columbine
- Goldenrod
- Indian Paintbrush
- Trillium
- Violet

Cream of the Crops

Wisconsin's principal agricultural products:

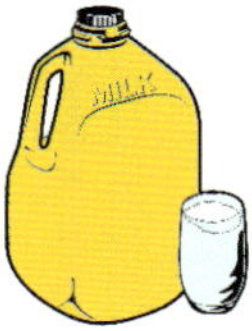

Milk

Beef Cattle

Hay

Cranberries

Oats

Snap Beans

Strawberries

Eggs

Potatoes

Onions

Hogs

Sweet Corn

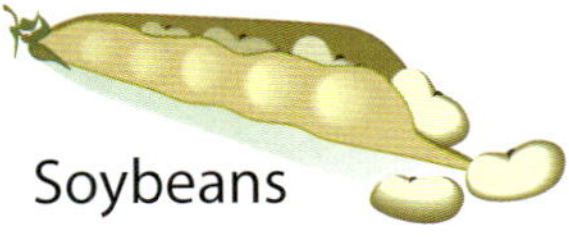

Soybeans

Apples

Firsts

1869
First commercial typewriter introduced at Kenosha.

1883
John Kohler invented the first bathtub by taking a pig trough, soldering legs on it, and coating the inside with white enamel.

1903
The first motorcycles were made by the Davidson brothers and William Harley.

1911
The Case Company introduced the first practical gas-powered tractor.

1960
143 foot-long (44-meters) muskie in Hayward built to house all the world records in freshwater fishing.

Festivals

Winterfest, held in Milwaukee in January

Chocolate Festival, held in Burlington in May

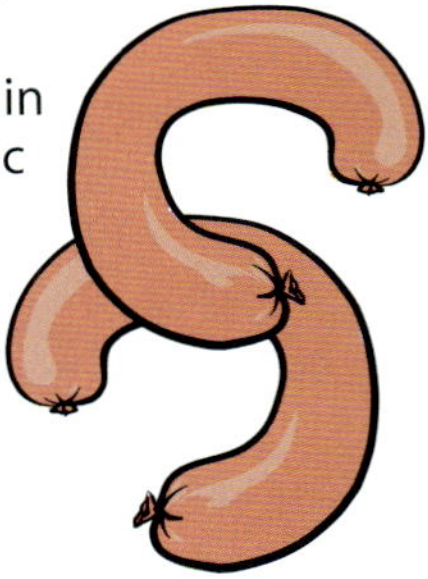

Summerfest, held in Milwaukee in June, is one of the world's largest music festivals. It lasts for 10 days!

German Fest, held in Milwaukee in July, where you can enjoy a bratwurst sausage!

Lumberjack World Championships, held in Hayward in July

Native American Fest, held in Milwaukee in September

Experimental Aircraft Association Expo, held in Oshkosh

Holidays

Calendar

Martin Luther King Day, *3rd Monday in January*

Presidents' Day, *3rd Monday in February*

St. Patrick's Day, *March 17*

Memorial Day, *last Monday in May*

Flag Day, *June 14*

Independence Day, *July 4*

Labor Day *1st Monday in September*

Columbus Day, *2nd Monday in October*

Veterans Day, *November 11*

Thanksgiving, *4th Thursday in November*

Christmas, *December 25*

The first Flag Day was started by a 19-year-old teacher in Waubeka. In 1885, a 10-inch flag with 38 stars was placed in a bottle on the teacher's desk. It took 31 years for Flag Day to become a national holiday.

Wisconsin's Wonderful Foods

- Bratwurst
- Sauerkraut
- Wienershnitzel
- Spaetzle
- Kielbasa
- Kringles
- Fried Cheese Curds
- Colby Cheese
- Brick Cheese
- Malted Milk
- Cranberry Ice Cream Sundae
- Chicken Booyah (stew)

Business & Trade

Wisconsin Works!

Besides the obvious dairy business, there are many other large industries in the state of Wisconsin. The leading industry groups are: industrial machinery and equipment; food and paper products; fabricated metal products; and printing and publishing. Although manufacturing is widely distributed, the city of Milwaukee accounts for more than one-third of the state's industrial income.

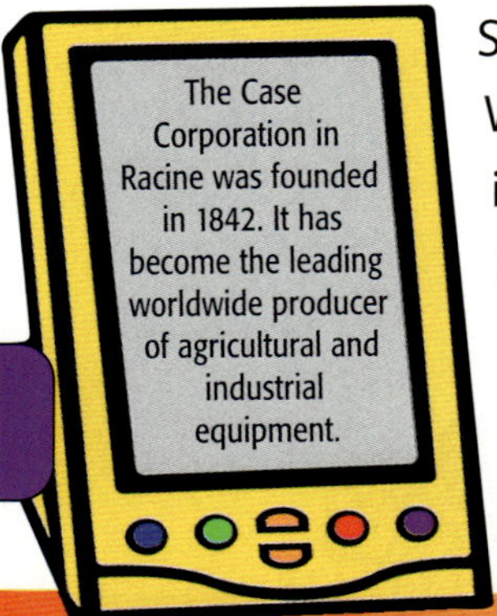

Some popular Wisconsin businesses include: OshKosh B'Gosh, SC Johnson Wax, Kraft, Kimberly-Clark; Parker Pens, and Pabst Brewery.

State Books & Websites

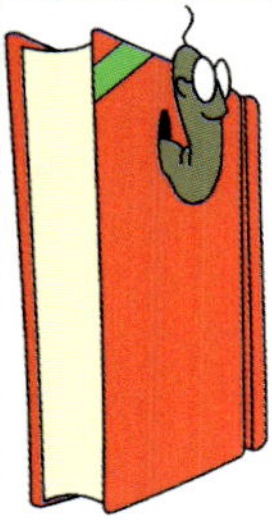

My First Book About Wisconsin
by Carole Marsh
America the Beautiful: Wisconsin
by Jean F. Blashfield
Wisconsin
by Gretchen Bratvold
Awesome Almanac: Wisconsin
by Margie Benson and Nancy Jacobson

Wisconsin Words to Know

Glossary Words

bratwurst: a German sausage
constitution: a document outlining the role of a government
dells: from the French word *dalles,* which means slabs or tiles. The dells are a series of rocky cliffs along the river.
endangered: in danger of becoming extinct
fort: a building with strong walls for defending against an enemy
founded: started or began
heritage: a way of life passed down from one's ancestors
immigrant: a person who comes to a new country to live
kringle: a popular flat, fruit-filled sweet pastry
population: the total number of people living in an area
reservations: public land set aside for special use, as in an Indian reservation

Wisconsin Spelling Bee

Here are some special Wisconsin-related words to learn! To take the Spelling Bee, have someone call out the words and you spell them aloud or write them on a piece of paper.

SPELLING WORDS		
	archaic	**Kenosha**
	badger	**Kinnickinnic**
	Ojibwa	**Outagamie**
	wienershnitzel	**walleye**
	Winnebago	**Manitou**
	Menominee	**Baraboo**
	Wausau	**Boscobel**
	Apostle	**territory**
	peninsula	**manufacturing**
	Rhinelander	
	escarpment	

About the Author

ABOUT THE AUTHOR...

CAROLE MARSH has been writing about Wisconsin for more than 20 years. She is the author of the popular Wisconsin State Stuff series for young readers and creator, along with her son, Michael Marsh, of "Wisconsin Facts and Factivities," a CD-ROM widely used in Wisconsin schools. The author of more than 100 Wisconsin books and other supplementary educational materials on the state, Marsh is currently working on a new collection of Wisconsin materials for young people. Marsh correlates her Wisconsin materials to the MODEL Academic Standards for Social Studies. Many of her books and other materials have been inspired by or requested by Wisconsin teachers and librarians.

The author dedicates this book to her husband, Bob Longmeyer, who has helped her with all the research ("and driving!") necessary to complete her more than 10,000 childrens' titles.